DEVELOPING WORLD

INDIA AND MUMBAI

JENNY VAUGHAN

W

DEVELOPING WORLD

INDIA AND MUMBAI

W
FRANKLIN WATTS
LONDON • SYDNEY

Franklin Watts

Published in 2016 by the Watts Publishing Group
An imprint of Hachette Children's Group
Part of the Watts Publishing Group
Carmelite House
50 Victoria Embankment

An Hachette UK company
www. hachette.co.uk
www.franklinwatts.co.uk

ISBN 978 1 4451 4954 7
Dewey number: 954.0532

Series Editor: Julia Bird
Series Advisor: Emma Epsley, geography teacher and consultant
Series Design: sprout.uk.com

Picture credits:
AF Archive/Alamy: 37tl. AJP/Shutterstock: front cover t. Alamy Celebrity/Alamy: 37tr. arindambanerjee/Shutterstock: 34t. Ajay Bhaskar/Dreamstime 28. Oleg D/Shutterstock: 20. Dario Diament/Shutterstock: 37b. Excel Media/Rex Features: 13t. Kevin Fletcher/Dreamstime: 38.f9photos/Shutterstock: 43b. Christopher Furlong/Getty Images: 39t. Anna Furman/Shutterstock: 39b. Gauravmasand/Dreamstime: 21b. gopixgo/ Shutterstock: 6. Nick Gray/Wikimedia Commons: 10. Jorg Hackemann/Shutterstock: 26. Nick Hanna/Alamy: 29b. Jaguar PS/Shutterstock: 36. Maurice Joseph/Almay: 27. Milind Ketkar/ Dreamstime.com: 21t. Lebrecht Music & Arts/Alamy: 35. LiteChoices/Shutterstock: 13b. Kistryn Malgorzata /Shutterstock: 19b. Matt McInnis/Dreamstime: 17t. Vladimir Meinik/ Shutterstock: 9t. Julia Milberger/istockphoto: 30b. Nice prospects-Prime/Alamy: 29b. OPIS Zagreb/Shutterstock: 30t. Christine Osborne Pictures/Alamy: 16. Pietrach/Dreamstime: 11t. Plus Lee/Shutterstock: 17b. Paul Prescott/Shutterstock: 22, 31. Project1photography/Dreamstime: 11c. Jean-Baptiste Rabouan/Alamy: 19t. Daniel Rao/istockphoto: 24. Daniel J. Rao/Shutterstock: 25. Fredrik Renander/Alamy: 23. Jeremy Richards/Shutterstock: 33. Samrat35/Dreamstime: 15t, 15b, 40. Sapsiwai/ Shutterstock: 11b. Sipa Press/Rex Features: 12. Nickolay Stanev/Shutterstock: front cover b, 8. Pavel Svobova/Shutterstock: 18. Pal Teravagimov/Shutterstock: 32. Aleksandaar Todorovic/Shutterstock: 21c. View Pictures/UIG/Getty Images: 34b. Ian Walker/Dreamstime: 7b. World History Archive/Alamy: 9b. Zeber/Shutterstock: 14, 42. Artur Zebrowski/Dreamstime: 41t.

Printed in Malaysia

DEVELOPING WORLD

INDIA AND MUMBAI

CONTENTS

LAND OF CONTRASTS

India is the seventh largest country in the world, and covers over three million square kilometres of south Asia. It is a land of huge contrasts. In the far north lies the world's highest mountain range, the Himalayas. Further south, the flat, fertile Indo-Gangetic Plain stretches from Pakistan in the west to Bangladesh in the east, and is made up largely of the Ganga (or Ganges) river basin. The Great Indian (or Thar) Desert forms a southern extension of the plain, stretching into Pakistan. Peninsular India juts out into the Indian Ocean, and has a varied, dramatic landscape with mountain ranges and hills.

The town of Darjiling (formerly Darjeeling) is in the Himalayas. The highest mountain in India, Kanchenjunga, can be seen in the background.

CLIMATE

Climate in India varies from region to region – the mountainous north, for example, has freezing winters, the Thar desert is very dry and the tropical south is lush and wet. India is described as having a 'monsoon climate', which means the seasons depend which way the wind is blowing. From mid-June to early October, winds from the Indian Ocean carry moisture across India, bringing rain. Between November and February, dry winds blow in from the interior of Asia. From March to June, and in October, there is little wind.

A CHANGING COUNTRY

India's fast-growing population is now an estimated 1.28 billion. By contrast, when India achieved independence from colonial rule in 1947, the population was about 350 million. Once extremely underdeveloped, since the 1990s India has been one of the world's fastest-growing economies. But while some people have become very wealthy, poverty remains a problem: an estimated quarter of the population lives on less than US $1.25 (80p) a day (the World Bank's benchmark of poverty).

POPULATION GROWTH (2000–2012)

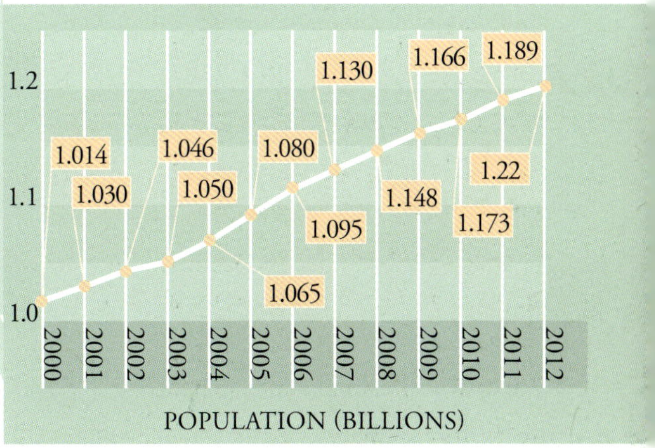

NEW AND OLD

Rapid development has brought better schools and medical care for many, but has also resulted in pollution, overcrowding and great inequalities between people. However, the traditional values of Indian family life and religion remain important.

India's city population is growing. Around 31% of Indians lived in cities in 2011 – set to rise to 35% by 2020.

SPOTLIGHT ON INDIA

AREA: 3,287,263 sq km • POPULATION: approx 1.28 billion (2015) • CAPITAL: New Delhi • LARGEST CITIES: Mumbai: 21.5 million; New Delhi: 21.7 million • LONGEST RIVER: The Ganga (2,510 km) • HIGHEST MOUNTAIN: Kanchenjunga (8,586 metres) • MAIN LANGUAGES: Hindi 41%, Bengali 8.1%, Telugu 7.2%, Marathi 7%, Tamil 5.9%, Urdu 5% • MAIN RELIGIONS: Hindu 80.5%, Muslim 13.4%, Christian 2.3%, Sikh 1.8% • NATURAL RESOURCES: petroleum, coal, natural gas, iron ore, copper, bauxite, ceramic clays, diamonds

PAST INTO PRESENT

The Presidential House in New Delhi, designed by British architect Edwin Landseer Lutyens, shows the British legacy in India.

ANCIENT INDIA

The first cities on the Indian subcontinent grew up over 4,000 years ago, in present-day Pakistan. India's main religion – now called Hinduism – developed around 3,000 years ago, possibly after settlers arrived from Central Asia.

FOREIGN INVADERS

Between around 320 and 1000 CE, after centuries of being small kingdoms, larger Indian empires grew up. In 1526, Muslim invaders set up the Mughal Empire in India. The British traded with the Mughals through the privately-owned East India Company. This eventually became more powerful than the Mughals, and even had its own army. In 1857, Indian soldiers in this army rebelled. Following this, the British government took direct control of India, though Indians continued to campaign for independence. From 1885, this struggle was led by the Indian National Congress, still a major political party today.

INDEPENDENCE AND AFTERWARDS

India won independence in 1947. With this came the 'partition' of the country into predominantly Hindu India and the largely Muslim Pakistan. As people from both communities fled across the new borders, violence left around a million people dead. Until 1972, Pakistan was divided into two parts: West and East Pakistan, with India located between them. In 1972, following a war between India and Pakistan, East Pakistan became independent Bangladesh – with India's support. West Pakistan remained simply Pakistan.

An Indian soldier on duty in Kashmir. Tensions between India and Pakistan, which go back to the partition, are especially acute in this region.

TENSIONS

Although they live in one of the world's fastest-growing economies, many Indians remain poor. This wealth gap dates partly from British rule, when development was designed more to make money for the rulers than the mass of the people. Many Indians also blame governments since independence for mismanaging the economy. Poverty, and tensions between Hindus and Muslims, have made Indian politics volatile, with occasional outbreaks of rioting and violence. Relations between India and Pakistan are strained and war has broken out several times – mostly over the region of Kashmir, which is claimed by both countries. This is especially dangerous, as both countries are now nuclear powers.

MAHATMA GANDHI

PEACEFUL PROTESTOR

Mahatma Gandhi is the most famous campaigner for Indian independence. He was born in 1869 in Gujarat and trained as a lawyer in London. As leader of the Indian National Congress, he led the campaign for independence and was imprisoned as a dangerous rebel, although he always rejected violence. Gandhi opposed the partition of India, and was assassinated by a Hindu extremist in 1948. Gandhi's belief in the importance of non-violent protest lives on today, and he is honoured by peace movements all over the world.

FOCUS ON MUMBAI

ISLAND CITY

Mumbai is the capital of the Indian state of Maharashtra. Originally called Bombay, it grew up on an island with that name off India's west coast. In 1995, the Maharashtra state government officially changed Bombay's name to Mumbai (a name some local people had always used), after a Hindu goddess, Mumba, who is especially important to the city. Re-naming was part of a move throughout India to change place names associated with British rule. Today, Mumbai is India's wealthiest and most populous city.

MUMBAI IN HISTORY

The area around Mumbai has been settled for thousands of years and was an important port as long ago as 1000 BCE. After a brief spell under Portuguese rule, the powerful British East India Company established control over the city. In the 1850s, cotton spinning and weaving mills were set up there. Trade flourished, especially during the US Civil War, when no cotton was exported from the USA, and Mumbai became wealthy.

MUMBAI TODAY

Although textiles are still important, Mumbai is now a centre for many other industries, including metals, chemicals, car-making and electronics. It is also the home of 'Bollywood', India's film hub (see page 36) and is India's financial centre.

The Haji Ali Dargah, a tomb and mosque. This famous Mumbai landmark is visited by people of all religions. It is linked to the city by a causeway and can only be reached at low tide.

CROWDED CITY

Being on an island means Mumbai has always been densely populated. By the end of the 19th century, it was already overcrowded. In the 1950s, it spread northwards after a causeway was built to a neighbouring island, Salsette. Today, the Mumbai Metropolitan Region takes in Mumbai and a number of satellite towns. It is one of the world's most populous cities, with over 21 million inhabitants – up from around 12 million in 1991. Mumbai's population density is estimated at between 25–30,000 people per square kilometre – one of the highest in the world.

A Mumbai street fruit and vegetable market. Mumbai has modern shops and supermarkets, but many people prefer to buy food from open-air markets.

A group of film extras pose on the set of an Indian-made movie. Mumbai is a centre for movie-making – and is often called 'Bollywood' – a mix of 'Bombay' and 'Hollywood'.

Chowpatty Beach, Mumbai. Mumbai has a number of beaches. This is its best known – and often one of the most crowded.

A DIVIDED DEMOCRACY

RIGHT TO VOTE

With around 1.28 billion inhabitants, India has over 17 per cent of the world's population. Around one out of six people on this planet lives in India. Only China has more people. But India, unlike China, is a democracy – the world's largest. Politicians are elected to run the country and India's 29 states. The oldest political party is the Indian National Congress. Its main rival, the BJP, is linked to the Hindu religion. Around 800 million Indians have the right to vote: that is, anyone over the age of 18 who is not 'mentally challenged' or a criminal.

POWER HOUSE

India has an elected president, but the real power lies with the prime minister, who is the leader of whichever party has the most members of parliament in the Lok Sabha (House of the People). This is one of two houses of parliament. The other is the Rajya Sabha (Council of States), whose members are elected by parliaments in each state.

LANGUAGE

Communication is vital to politics and the economy, but this is made difficult by the fact that India has hundreds of tribal and national groups in India, each with their own languages, dialects and cultures. To make communication easier, Hindi has been made a national language. English, a second official language, is widely spoken in business.

Indian voters queue at a polling station at the 2009 general election. There were 714 million eligible voters, with 828,804 polling stations.

UNEQUAL WEALTH

Although India is home to some of the world's richest people, an estimated one in six people in India is hungry. Poverty is unevenly spread. In the northern state of Chhattisgarh in 2012, for example, around 40 per cent of people lived in poverty, while in the southern state of Kerala, it was only 7 per cent. This is partly because some areas have better resources than others. It is also because foreign and domestic investment favours some parts of India more than others. Deep divisions between rich and poor can encourage resentment, violence and crime.

Children often have to contribute to family income. This girl is collecting cotton waste from a factory to sell for a small price.

WHAT COUNTS AS POOR?

The World Bank measures absolute poverty as less than $1.25 (80p) per day per person to live on. The most recent figures for world poverty levels from the World Bank were estimated as:

• Tanzania 43.4% • Bangladesh: 43.3% • India: 23.6%
• Pakistan: 12.7% • China: 6.3% • Mexico: 1%

India's official 2012 measure of poverty is 33 rupees (33 pence) a day in towns and cities, and 27 rupees (27 pence) in rural areas. This puts the proportion of people living in poverty at around 22 per cent. But critics say India's measure is too low. At the World Bank measure of poverty at $1.25 a day, the number of people living in poverty is higher (nearly a third of the population) but at $2 a day (still very little money), it was nearly 60 per cent.

COMMUNICATIONS

Good communications and transport links are vital in a country as large as India and are all the more important as India grows as a world economic power.

ON THE ROAD

India has around 4.1 million kilometres of roads, but only around half of them are paved. Unpaved roads are easily damaged in bad weather, making travel difficult. However, car ownership in India is growing fast. Around 2.5 per cent of households had a car in 2001, but this rose to an estimated 6 per cent by 2015.

AIR AND RAIL LINKS

For millions, traditional forms of transport, such as hand-drawn rickshaws and bullock carts, are all that is available. Even public transport is a problem in isolated villages, where a bus stop may be several hours' walk away. By contrast, the better-off can use air travel. India's domestic passenger numbers reached over 67.3 million in 2014 – up from only about 26 million in 2006. Rail has always been important in India's economy, with around 65,000 km of routes, carrying around 20 million passengers and 2.5 tonnes of freight a day.

Auto-rickshaws or 'tuk-tuks' are a common sight on India's roads. These three-seater vehicles are very economical to run.

A man in a rural area of Madhya Pradesh state, in central India, talks on a mobile phone. Mobiles are very popular in areas where there are not enough landlines.

KEEPING IN TOUCH

India's first telegraph systems were set up in the 1850s. Landline telephones arrived in the 1880s. However, as in many developing countries, mobile phones are more practical, as they do not need expensive wiring to support them. The first mobiles reached India in the 1990s. By 2015 about a billion people were using mobiles. The World Bank estimates that 18 people out of every 100 use the Internet: those without access at home use workplaces or Internet cafés.

India's beautiful beaches attract tourists from all over the world.

ARRIVALS FROM ABROAD

Nearly 7 million tourists a year arrive in India, mostly from the US, but also from Europe and other Asian countries. Mumbai and Delhi airports together bring in almost half of all international arrivals. In 2013, tourism contributed an estimated US $18 billion to India's economy – around 6.8 per cent of GDP. Tourism can help to support heritage sites, such as ancient temples and wildlife parks, which might otherwise be lost to development. But tourism has a down side: it can damage the environment, use up scarce land and water and distort local culture as people adapt traditional art and crafts to please visitors.

LIVING STANDARDS

When it comes to how people live, there are huge differences between the rich and the poor, like everything else in India.

HEALTHCARE

India has some world-class private hospitals – so good that people from richer countries attend them for treatment, which is often cheaper than in the West. For the poor, there are state-run clinics and programmes for vaccinating children against dangerous diseases, and charities run clinics in the slums and rural areas. But these are not sufficient for India's booming population, and paying for private care – which many Indians must do – can push families into poverty.

ELECTRICITY

As far back as 2003, the Indian government set a goal of 'power for all' by 2012. But around a quarter to a half of Indians still do not have access to mains electricity. The situation is worse in villages, but even in cities, supplies are unreliable. Rapid development has put a strain on India's ageing supply network, and there are frequent power cuts. One, in July 1012, left half the country without electricity, bringing public transport and factories to a standstill. The system needs modernising, and India needs new power stations. But it is not always easy to get people to agree to these being built – especially when it involves damming rivers for hydroelectric power. It also has to be paid for. India's government has little money to spend as so many people are too poor to pay much – if any – tax.

A rural vaccination clinic in Goa, India. Indian parents are encouraged to have their babies immunised against a range of diseases, including polio, diphtheria and measles.

WATER AND SANITATION

Twenty-five or so years ago, a third of Indians had no access to safe drinking water. Today, things are better – with safe water available to around 90 per cent of people, according to a report from UNICEF and the World Health Organization. But that still leaves many without clean water, and access is often from shared taps some distance away. In rural areas, people may have to walk long distances to wells, which may not always be clean. One of the biggest dangers to health is from water polluted with human or animal waste. Proper toilet facilities are also a major problem. Only 60 per cent of city-dwellers and 24 per cent of people in rural areas have access to any kind of toilet. In city slums, many ditches are open sewers running between houses.

An Indian mother and daughter fetch water at the rural community well in Khuri, a village in Rajasthan.

EDUCATION

Children in Darjiling, in northern India, on their way home from school. In rural areas, children may have to walk several kilometres to and from school.

Good education is essential for any country that wants to compete in the modern world. Providing this is one of greatest challenges facing India.

GOING TO SCHOOL

In 2009, India made education free and compulsory for all children from six to 14. Estimates of those enrolled suggest that over 90 per cent of children have a place at a school, but this is not the whole story. In some communities, children may have to work instead of study or, often in the case of girls, be expected to help at home. In rural areas, there can be the issue that schools are simply too far away for children to reach easily. By secondary level, estimates of children enrolled had dropped to around 70 per cent – slightly more for boys than girls.

AROUND INDIA

Education levels between the different Indian states vary. As with fighting poverty, Kerala, in the south, does well, with over 90 per cent literacy, compared with about 64 per cent in Bihar. Everywhere, girls fare worse than boys in education as, in many more traditional households, they are held back in education, kept at home and encouraged to marry early.

FOREIGN CAMPUSES

Several foreign universities have set up partnerships with Indian universities to attract foreign students without asking them to leave their home countries. Lancaster University, for example, works in partnership with a GD Goenka World Institute, near Delhi. US universities operating in India include Virginia Tech, which opened a research centre in Tamil Nadu in 2014.

BRAIN DRAIN

India has a long tradition of losing its highest qualified professionals to the US, Europe and Australia, where there are better career opportunities and higher wages. The Indian government is trying to tackle this by offering higher-paid fellowships to new graduates and to scientists who have settled abroad, hoping that they will return to India and take up posts there.

A computer class at Mayo College, Ajmer, in Rajasthan. This private school was founded in 1870 by the British Viceroy (ruler) of India, Lord Mayo, for the sons of Indian princes.

UNIVERSITY AND COLLEGE

India has some high quality universities and colleges whose history goes back over 100 years. These have played an important part in educating India's politicians, scientists and business people. The Indian government believes that higher education is vital in keeping the country's economy growing. Around a quarter of young Indians are enrolled in tertiary education (universities and colleges) and the government hopes to increase this to 30 per cent by 2020. Many new universities and colleges have been set up – some by overseas universities building campuses in India (see panel).

The University of Mumbai, founded in 1857, is one of India's oldest and most important universities.

FOCUS ON MUMBAI

LIVING IN MUMBAI

Life in Mumbai presents many of the same advantages and problems as the rest of India. These play out against the backdrop of a busy, heavily populated, developing city.

HIGH RISE VS SLUMS

A 27-storey house, belonging to a wealthy Indian businessman, stands out against Mumbai's skyline. It is not the only extraordinarily luxurious home in Mumbai, as the city is home to many incredibly rich people. Yet, by contrast, more than 60 per cent of Mumbai's inhabitants live on just a few hundred pounds a year, in crowded slums without clean drinking water or proper sanitation.

A MIDDLE CLASS

Like many other Indian cities, Mumbai has a growing middle class that earns less than those in similar jobs in Europe and the US, but still may be able to afford luxury items such as televisions. Some estimate that as many as 50 million Indians are part of this class, which, if the Indian economy continues to expand at its current rate, could grow by as much as ten times within the next ten years.

Living space is at a premium in Mumbai so rents are high. Many middle-class families still live ageing blocks called 'chawls'. These are often overcrowded and in need of repair, but give extended family members a chance to live close to each other at low rents.

MOVING MILLIONS

Like many Indians, few Mumbaikars (inhabitants of Mumbai) own cars, but this is increasing fast, with 170 thousand motor vehicles being registered in 2013–4. Estimates are that there will be over two million vehicles on Mumbai's roads by 2030 – up from around 720,000 in 2014. But most people – around 90 per cent – rely on public transport. The local railway system transports just over seven million commuters a day.

Others use buses, while richer passengers can travel by auto-rickshaw. Ferries operate between the islands. In 2014, a new metro system opened, which should relieve some of the crowds on roads and trains. In its first three weeks it carried 7.6 million commuters.

Yet in India old and new live side by side – hand-drawn rickshaws and bullock carts are still commonplace in Mumbai's streets.

Tuk tuks in Mumbai. These vehicles add to the pollution in the city's air, but recently, less polluting engines have been developed to help reduce this problem.

Nearly a quarter of a million people travelled on the sleek, new Mumbai Metro on its first day of operation.

Dharavi is a huge Mumbai slum, almost in the centre of the city. Some estimates are that nearly a million people live there, mostly in illegal settlements with very poor sanitation.

A luxurious apartment building on Mumbai's exclusive Marine Drive, near Chowpatty Beach. Only the very rich can afford to live in buildings like these.

ECONOMIC POWERHOUSE

FULL SPEED AHEAD

India's GDP (Gross Domestic Product – the value of everything it produces) has grown at an average of 7 per cent since 1997. By contrast, in the US and Europe, GDP has barely grown at all. Recently, however, India's growth has begun to slow down.

PAST AND PRESENT

In the past, India's industry was mostly smallscale, such as pot-making for local use. These industries still exist, but others have become far more important. Textiles – cloth and clothing – make up over a quarter of India's income from exports, and it is the second largest textile producer after China. Major retailers, including labels such as Gucci, Gap and Calvin Klein, use Indian factories. Unfortunately, all over the world, this industry has a bad reputation, often relying on sweatshops (see panel), where workers put in long hours for low wages, in overcrowded conditions. The best importers inspect factories regularly to make sure that conditions are acceptable.

SWEATSHOPS

Some campaigners accuse India of being one of the worst places in the world for 'sweatshops', where children – often as young as six – are employed. In 2012, the Indian government outlawed employing children under 14, but is under pressure to allow child labour in family businesses.

Men at work in a textile factory. This industry provides a great boost to India's exports, but people may work long hours for little pay.

Two young Information Technology workers in Bangalore. Around a third of India's IT professionals work in Bangalore.

TECHNOLOGICAL REVOLUTION

In the 1990s, the Indian government decided to prioritise the growth of its software industry. To make up for India's often unreliable telephone system, the government invested in high-quality satellite communications. Bangalore (also called Bengaluru) in south India became the main centre of the industry, as it was already a base for electronic companies and research institutions for India's military. The industry soon took off. Today, many multinational electronics companies have Indian design and development centres, and successful Indian companies such as Infosys and Wipro Ltd have grown up and developed alongside huge software multinationals such as Microsoft.

OTHER INDUSTRIES

Tata Motors, a world-leading motor manufacturer, has its head office in Mumbai and factories throughout India. It was set up after World War II to make commercial vehicles, and began making passenger cars in the 1990s, including the Tata Nano, an inexpensive car for the home market. Tata has expanded over the years to take in foreign companies, such as Jaguar LandRover in the UK.

CALLING INDIA

Over the last 15 years, India has developed as a successful base for call centres, as international companies such as banks and mobile phone companies looked to cut costs by employing Indian workers to staff their helpdesks. However, this once-booming industry may now be on the wane. Some global businesses, such as the banking group Santander, and parts of Barclays bank, have relocated their centres back to their countries of origin to improve customer service. Other countries, such as the Philippines, are also emerging as cheaper call centre hubs.

AGRICULTURE

Despite its expanding industrial sector, India is still at heart a rural country, and at least half of all workers are involved in farming. Agriculture makes up around a fifth of India's GDP.

SMALL FARMS

Indians spend around 25 per cent of their income on food. Most food comes from smallscale, mainly subsistence farms, where farmers grow food for their families, alongside a little extra to sell. Crops include vegetables, such as rice and corn, fruit, such as bananas and mangoes, and staples such as rice and wheat.

CHANGING WAYS

Until recently, only a few crops, such as tea, coffee and cotton, were major exports. Now, other crops are exported. In Punjab, for example, large amounts of wheat are grown to be sold internationally. In 2013–4, India produced over 93.5 million tonnes of wheat, making it the third largest wheat producer after the EU and China.

LIVESTOCK

Cattle are sacred to Hindus. Many people keep just a few cows so, although there are few large herds, collectively they amount to nearly a third of all the cattle in the world at around 300 million. They are kept for milk, rather than meat. Poultry is also kept on small farms for eggs and meat.

Women picking tea on a plantation in Assam, north-west India. India produces around 30 per cent of the world's tea, employing more than two million people.

FISHING

Around 3.5 million people in villages along the Indian coastline earn a living from fishing, and millions more depend on the industry. But it is under threat. As larger, powered craft take over from small boats, there is a serious danger of over-fishing, which could lead to the collapse of fish stocks, making it impossible for fishing communities to survive. Campaigners believe it is vital that the Indian government finds a way to prevent this from happening.

Inland, the government is encouraging fish-farming in areas such as West Bengal, where there is plenty of fresh water. Around three and a half million tonnes of fish is produced in inland India – more than half of it now from farms. In the future, India could expand this three times over.

Fishing off the Malabar coast in south-western India. Today, small traditional fishing boats are facing competition from large mechanised ships.

EMPLOYMENT IN INDIA

India's total workforce is around 480 million. Many people (perhaps over 80 per cent) work in the 'informal sector' – that is, outside government control. This makes it hard to know how many people are employed in different ways, but estimates are:

agriculture 47% • services 28% • industry 25%

FARMING CHALLENGES

Subsistence farming is much more challenging than large-scale agriculture. One stroke of bad luck, such as a flood or drought, or an outbreak of illness among the livestock, and a family or whole community can go hungry.

THE 'GREEN REVOLUTION'

Indian farmers tackle the insecurities they face by adopting more modern farming methods. Many now buy and plant high yielding seeds instead of using grain they have saved from previous years. They also apply chemical fertilisers, as well as using animal dung, to enrich soil, and ox-drawn ploughs are giving way to tractors. This change in farming, which began in the 1960s, is called 'the Green Revolution' and has massively increased food production.

THE DOWNSIDE

New technology is not always good news. Older seed varieties and traditional crops are more resistant to drought and do not cost much to grow. The high price of new seeds and artificial fertilisers can lead farmers into debt and many thousands of farmers have been forced to leave the countryside for the cities to make money.

LAND RIGHTS

Many rural people are Adivasi, descendents of the earliest people to live in India. They may always have lived in an area, but it is hard to prove their right to be there. Big building projects such as mines and reservoirs may try to throw them off the land. A law passed in 2013 allowed land to be acquired only if local people agreed. But this is under attack, and the fight goes on.

Maize (corn) being transported in Rajasthan, north-west India. Getting food from farms to the people who need it is often a problem, and too often, crops go to waste.

Adivasi women at a market in Orissa, eastern India.

OUR LAND!

Chembakolli village is in the Nilgiri Hills in Tamil Nadu. The people there are Adivasi. In 1988, the people of the Nilgiri Hills joined a campaign to get traditionally held land back, and in 1990, they succeeded. Today, many Chembakolli people are still poor, but they live in concrete houses with good roofs, and the children can go to school. They have their own tea plantation, and sell tea all over the world.

FOCUS ON MUMBAI

WORKING CITY

Indians call Mumbai 'the land of opportunities'. Its history as a trading centre goes back as far as the 1600s, when it exported textiles, jewellery, cotton and rice.

MODERN MUMBAI

Mumbai is the commercial capital of India, and its centre of finance and banking. It is one of the world's top ten centres of commerce and contributes around a quarter of India's industrial output. Many large foreign companies have offices in Mumbai, including the communications and technology giant Siemens.

Other industries include software companies, pharmaceutical manufacturers and 'heavy' industry, such as making products of steel and rubber, while the long tradition of textile and garment manufacture still survives. All this offers work to millions – some in factories and offices, but many others work in the informal sector.

INFORMAL WORK

The informal sector is made up of people the government has little contact with. They do not pay tax and are often self-employed. They may work in workshops, making pottery, clothing or leather goods, drive rickshaws, or get casual work as labourers. Often, they support extended families far away in the villages.

High-rise buildings are a way to provide homes for the millions who live in Mumbai. These are luxury flats – too expensive for most people.

Huge amounts of money can be generated in these smaller areas of industry. Some estimate that the economic output from Mumbai's Dharavi slum (see p.21) could reach US$1 billion. Most trading is done within the slum and nearby, but some craft workers have started to trade online, selling goods such as clothing and handicrafts.

Every day in Mumbai, about 5,000 deliverymen carry around 200,000 'tiffin tins' (containers of home-cooked lunches) to factories and offices.

The Mumbai head office of the State Bank of India. This is just one of the major banks in Mumbai.

These pots are made in the Dharavi slum and sold for everyday use all over India.

ENVIRONMENTAL COSTS

India's development has brought jobs and wealth to many, but it comes at a cost for the environment.

WATER SHORTAGE

Modern farming methods have helped provide food for India's growing population, but this needs huge amounts of water. In the Punjab region so much water is used to grow wheat and rice that the aquifer (underground water) levels are dropping, affecting vital supplies. Mining and quarrying provide important fuel and building materials, but drain water away. Elsewhere, bridges and dams block rivers. The need for water and hydroelectric power stations has led to more and more dams being built. These are controversial, as land where people once lived and farmed is flooded.

SOIL

Deforestation is a major problem. Often, it is the result of logging – trees being chopped down for timber. Land is also cleared for farming. Poor farming methods, which include using too much chemical fertiliser, can damage the soil, leaving it bare. As it washes away, rivers become clogged up and the dangers of flooding increase. Wind can also blow soil away, creating deserts and ruining crops. Around half of India's land surface is affected by soil loss. For India to continue to develop, it is important to educate farmers to look after the soil. There are a number of government initiatives that are trying to help farmers manage the land better, and there are laws against illegal logging.

The Tehri Dam reservoir in northern India. Although it can produce massive amounts of power and water, the dam has resulted in local people losing their land and livelihoods.

When forests are cut down, wildlife and people who depend on forest plants both suffer. The soil may also be washed away, so that it is no longer good for food production.

WATER POLLUTION

India's rivers are often highly polluted. The Ganga, sacred to the Hindu religion, flows for over 2,500 km, supplying water to over 400 million people. More than two-thirds of sewage generated daily in 118 towns that lie along the Ganga is discharged into the river untreated – estimates range from two billion litres a day upwards. Agricultural waste and poisonous chemicals from factories add to the problem. Pollution is now thought to be 3,000 times over the limit suggested by the World Health Organization (WHO) as 'safe'. However, local authorities and the national government are acting together to try to clean up the river. It is a huge task.

AIR

India's rapid development has resulted in a big increase in its greenhouse gas emissions, the gases believed to be responsible for climate change. It is estimated that India's greenhouse gas emissions rose by 58 per cent between 1994 and 2007, making India the fourth largest producer of greenhouse gases after China, the US and the EU. The WHO names Delhi as having the most polluted atmosphere of any city in the world. Suggestions for tackling this include raising fuel taxes to discourage traffic and improving public transport.

Smog hangs over the city of Delhi. Scientists warn that the level of pollution in Delhi is dangerous to people's health.

RELIGION AND CASTE

For most Indians, religion is an important part of their lives, whichever faith they belong to.

THREAT TO TRADITION

Hinduism is the religion of the largest number of Indians. For devout Hindus, who reject material wealth, rapid development can seem alarming. The fact that India is officially a secular (non-religious) state is only partly accepted by traditionalists. Many view the growing modernisation of everyday life – especially among women (see page 41) – as a threat to long-held beliefs and values.

CASTE

The caste system is a social structure linked to Hinduism. People are born into their caste, which can affect every part of their lives – where they live, who they marry, what jobs they do, and much more.

Discrimination on the grounds of caste is illegal, but it still happens. It is beginning to break down, but not fast enough for the 'dalits' (once known as 'untouchables') – the 16 or so per cent of Indians at the bottom of the caste system, who are often found doing the worst-paid jobs. Affirmative action has gone some way to help, but dalits have seen little of the positive side of Indian development.

ISLAM

Even after India achieved independence, when millions fled to Pakistan for safety, many Muslims remained there. They now make up around 14 per cent of the population. Muslims suffer discrimination in today's India. Nearly a third are classed as poor, even by the Indian government standards, and, like the dalits, are often excluded from India's race to development.

Hindu pilgrims bathe in the River Ganga in the holy city of Varanasi in northern India. Devout Hindus hope to visit the city at least once in a lifetime.

Dalit children at work stitching footballs. Dalits traditionally work in 'impure' jobs, such as with leather (considered unclean because of the association with killing cows), butchery and with waste.

RIVALRY

Rivalry between the Muslims and Hindus is centuries old, dating from the earliest Mughal invasions. The bloodshed at partition stemmed from this rivalry, and made it worse. Both religions have fundamentalist wings, which can inflame inter-communal violence (violence between different communities). One of the worst events in memory took place in 1992, when riots all over India left more than 2,000 people dead after militant Hindus destroyed a mosque in Ayodhya, Uttar Pradesh. There have been many other similar events since, all bringing instability to the country and dividing the population.

Indian Muslims at prayer at the Jama Masjid, the most important mosque in Old Delhi.

FAMILY TIES

For Indians of all religions, family is deeply important. It means that people believe family members must care for each other and share their wealth. But it can also lead to nepotism – unfairly favouring family members in employment and other opportunities. This can be a threat to development, as it may exclude talented people from the economy.

THE ARTS

In the past, Indian art was mainly linked to religion. India's beautiful temples, mosques and other religious monuments still attract millions of visitors every year. India's literature, too, was often rooted in religion.

GMS Grande Palladium in Mumbai. This new office block was designed by Malik Architecture – one of the country's top firms of architects.

ARCHITECTURE

By contrast, India today has plenty of fine modern architecture. Much reflects India's role as a rapidly developing, modern country. These include public buildings, airport terminals and innovative office buildings – such as the GMS Grande Palladium in Mumbai (right). However, experts warn that India's infrastructure – its roads and power supply – must continue to improve if modern construction is to succeed. Some critics also say that it is also important to find ways of building 20 million or more affordable houses needed in India's cities, where many people still live in slums and other poor accommodation.

A scene from the Ramayana *is acted out at a theatre in Hyderabad.*

THE WRITTEN WORD

Ancient Hindu epics, the *Ramayana, Mahabharata* and *Bhagavad Gita* were written around 2,500 years ago, and tell the stories of ancient gods and heroes. They are still read, and made into films, plays and poetry. But in India today much new literature is written in English, and available to readers all over the world. This includes the work of writers such as novelists Salman Rushdie, Anita Desai and Arundhati Roy. All these writers have played an important part in introducing modern India to the rest of the world, while Indian drama is gradually finding its way onto the stages of Europe and the US.

Vasu Dixit, of Indian band Swarathma, performing at the Larmer Tree Festival in the UK. Swarathma is a folk 'fusion' band based in Bangalore that combines folk tunes and Western sounds.

MUSIC

As with most Indian art, music has a long history, and was first played in temples and palaces. Classical Indian music is still played today, as are traditional instruments such as the sitar. But like so much in India, ancient traditions are now often combined with modern influences to create a unique mix that also includes rock and pop, for example, by adding a modern beat to traditional Hindi songs.

AN INDIAN ARTIST

There are many world-class modern artists and sculptors living and working in India today. Atul Dodiya (born 1959), who was born and lives in Mumbai, studied at the city's Sir Jamsetjee Jeejebhoy School of Art (Sir JJ School of Art). His work includes paintings and installations, often inspired by Mumbai's most famous product – Bollywood films (see page 36).

FOCUS ON MUMBAI

MEDIA GIANT

Mumbai's media industry is huge, with many Indian radio and television stations based there, as well as national and local newspapers.

PRINT AND BROADCASTING

Mumbai has its own magazines and newspapers, along with local editions of national papers, such as the *Times of India*. Publications appear online as well as in print. There are numerous local radio stations, including eight on FM. India's national public radio company Akashvani (also called All India Radio) – one of the world's biggest broadcasters – has several local Mumbai stations. Radio is especially important in a country where many people cannot read.

Around 60 per cent of households in the state of Maharashtra (in which Mumbai is situated) have TV sets and can watch over a hundred television channels in a range of languages, mostly carried by three main cable networks. Television is also available online. Doordarshan, the national television broadcaster, has two free terrestrial channels.

SPORT AND MEDIA

Media plays an important part in India's favourite sport – cricket. The television rights are controlled by the Board of Control of Cricket in India (BCCI) – the world's richest governing body, worth around US$ 295 million. Mumbai's own team – the Mumbai Indians – has millions of fans (perhaps as many as six million) worldwide.

BOLLYWOOD

The entire Indian entertainment and media industry is set to earn over US $35 million a year by 2018. Perhaps the best-known form of Indian media is its massive film industry – expected to bring in around US$ 4.5 billion annually in 2016. 'Bollywood' produces hundreds of films each year, and India makes more films than any other country. These are watched all over the world, wherever the 25 million or so Indian diaspora (see page 38) live.

Hrithik Roshan is one of the biggest Bollywood stars. Here he is pictured at the Cannes Film Festival, with Uruguayan actress Bárbara Mori.

The 2008 hit film Slumdog Millionaire, *set and filmed in Mumbai, brought Indian cinema to a worldwide audience.*

A roadside fruit-seller in Mumbai reads one of the city's many newspapers.

Sachin Tendulkar, the Mumbai-based former Indian cricket captain, was one of the greatest cricketers ever. He retired from cricket in 2013.

INDIA IN THE MODERN WORLD

India's role in the world is changing as its economy, people and culture continue to make more and more of an impact.

THE DIASPORA

The Indian diaspora (people of Indian origin living in other countries) is huge – probably around 25 million. Migration began during British rule, when many poor Indians were encouraged (or forced by extreme poverty) to travel to distant parts of the world. Once there, they were often bound by unfair contracts called 'indentures' to remain, more or less as slaves. As a result, there are longstanding communities of people of Indian origin in Africa, the Caribbean and many other places. These grew as their families joined them.

NEW HOMES

In the 20th century, large numbers of Indians migrated to Britain, the US and Australia. With few opportunities at home, many took the opportunity to settle in wealthier parts of the world, where wages were much higher than at home. The first arrivals were mostly men, but later, their families joined them, and new communities of people of Indian origin grew up.

People of Indian origin living in London celebrate Holi, the Hindu festival of colours.

BIG BUSINESS

India's 100 richest people have amassed US $346 billion between them. Many operate all over the world, such as Lakshmi Mittal, head of the world's largest steelmaking company, with employees in 60 countries. Mittal, who is based in London, is the second richest Indian after Mumbai-based Mukesh Ambani, who has made a fortune in oil and gas. These wealthy businesses grew up in an India that is becoming five or six per cent richer every year. Although this rate has been slowing down, this is still a huge contrast with the economies of Europe and the US, where growth has been very limited. As India's economy expands, many European and American businesses are looking to it as a new market for their goods and services.

This sculpture was designed for the London 2012 Olympics by the Indian-born British sculptor, Anish Kapoor. It was mostly funded by ArcelorMittal, whose chairman is the Indian billionaire, Lakshmi Mittal.

TRADITIONAL BELIEFS

Even while Indian business is booming and India's scientists, writers and other skilled people are making an impact in the world, India remains a land of ancient tradition. As India's people have settled in the rest of the world they have brought with them ancient beliefs, such as their traditional Ayurvedic herbal medicine, and stress-reducing techniques such as meditation and yoga, all of which have become popular in the West.

Yoga originated in India. It is now practised throughout the world, as a means of seeking inner peace.

WOMEN IN INDIA

A couple celebrate their marriage in Kolkota, West Bengal. Most Indians still support the traditional belief that a marriage should be arranged by the couple's parents.

As India changes, the position of women in society reflects the divide between long-held tradition and modern development.

SUCCESS STORIES

Many Indian women have made remarkable achievements. A woman – Indira Gandhi – became prime minister as long ago as 1966. India has also had a woman president, Pratibha Devisingh Patil (2007 to 2012). Indian women have been successful in many other areas of work and industry. India has the largest number of professionally qualified women in the world, with more female doctors, scientists and professors than the United States.

DOWRIES

In Indian society, traditionally, sons are valued more highly than daughters. A boy, it is believed, will support his parents one day, but a girl will join another family on marriage and her in-laws may demand money on marriage (a dowry). Dowries were made illegal in the 1960s, but this has never been strictly enforced. The pressure of providing a dowry drives many families into debt – an estimated 80 per cent of bank loans in India are used to finance dowry demands. There are even cases of brides being murdered for their dowries by greedy in-laws.

GENDER IMBALANCE

At worst, a family may opt to abort an unborn daughter rather than face poverty. As estimated 8 million unborn girls were aborted in India between 2002 and 2012. As a result, in 2011, for every 1,000 boys under the age of six, there were just 914 girls. As well as being a humanitarian tragedy, if this gender imbalance continues, a generation of Indian men will be unable to marry and have families. The government is trying to tackle this by banning doctors from revealing an unborn baby's sex, and by subsidising girls' higher education.

SCHOOLING

Girls suffer in education, too (see page 18). The United Nations children's organisation, UNICEF estimates that although the literacy rate for young men between 18–24 is nearly 90 per cent, it is only just over 74 per cent for young women. However, attitudes are changing as people realise that educating girls benefits whole families in terms of health, education and earning power. There is an Indian saying that 'when you educate a woman, you educate a family'.

Education for girls still lags behind boys', but there are many pressure groups, as well as government policies, to encourage parents to send their daughters to school.

ROLE OF WOMEN

There are still tensions about the position of women. Modern Indian women who go out to work may be treated with hostility and even violence by traditionally-minded people (both men and women) who cling to the old belief that they should be treated as the property of their father or husbands.

A SHOCKING STORY

In December 2012, a young woman was raped and murdered on a bus in Delhi. Massive street demonstrations followed as Indians found their voice to protest against violence against women. They protested about the urgent need to solve the problem of overcoming traditional attitudes to women that could allow men to think they could behave like this. Unless this happens, campaigners say, India cannot call itself a modern country.

CHANGING TIMES

Children in Agra. Since 2003, infant mortality in India has dropped from 60 per 1,000 births in 2003 to 44 in 2011, thanks to public education programmes.

India certainly has challenges to tackle, but there are many people working to overcome them, and positive signs for the future.

POPULATION

Some estimate that by 2050, India will have a population of around 1.6 billion. This is challenging, but it could be worse. Population growth is slowing. Back in 1950, Indian women had around six children each. Now that average is slightly less than three. This is largely the result of better healthcare and education.

CORRUPTION

Anther enduring problem in India is corruption and the culture of giving bribes, for example when businesses pay public officials to treat their businesses favourably. Much corrupt money actually leaves India altogether – an estimated US $94.76 billion left the country in 2012. Sums this size slow down India's development. Public anger at the level of corruption led to an anti-corruption political party being set up, which won control of the city of Delhi in local elections in 2015.

THE NEXT FRONTIER

India has its own space programme, the Indian Space Research Organisation (ISRO), which was founded as long ago as 1969. In 2014 it completed a successful satellite mission to Mars with the Mangalyaan satellite, The same year, it tested a rocket carrying a module for a crew (though without anyone aboard). The ISRO regularly sends satellites into space for other countries – including five for the UK in 2015.

GREEN TECHNOLOGY

India has many environmental problems, but much is being done to tackle them, from projects to clean up the River Ganga to plans to reduce greenhouse gas emissions. In 2015, Indian Prime Minister announced that it was hoped to encourage investment of US$ 100 billion in solar energy over the next few years. This will be vital for a country that will soon be the most heavily populated in the world.

A remote road in Himachal Pradesh, in northern India. Preserving India's unique environment is one of its biggest challenges for the future.

GLOSSARY

Adivasi tribes of people descended from those whose ancestors lived in India in prehistoric times. They make up around 8 per cent of the Indian population
agriculture farming
aquifer underground rock that contains water
assassinate to kill someone, usually a public or political figure
Ayurvedic the traditional Hindu system of medicine, using diet, herbal treatment and breathing exercises
brain drain when skilled and educated people leave a country to work abroad, usually for better opportunities or more money
caste a traditional Indian system of dividing up society. The four main castes are: Brahmin (priests), warriors, traders and workers. People outside this system are known as dalits. They were once called 'untouchables'
causeway a raised pathway that crosses water
communications getting things or messages from one place to another. Railways and roads are forms of transport communications. Sending messages by telephone, computer or broadcasting are telecommunications
compulsory required by law
corruption being dishonest in business or in government – for example, by taking bribes
deforestation clearing away of trees
democracy a form of government in which citizens have a say in the decisions that affect their lives
development growing or advancing. A country is often described as developing when it is moving from traditional forms of agriculture and small-scale industry to more modern forms of both
dialect a form of a language found in a certain place, or among certain people. For example, English is a single language, but there are many different dialects of it
diaspora the spread of people away from their country of origin
dowry an amount of money and/ or property given by a wife to her husband on marriage
export to sell goods or services to another country
extra someone who appears in the background of a film or TV programme
fertiliser a chemical added to soil to make crops grow better
fish farming to breed fish for sale
freight goods carried in bulk
GDP (Gross Domestic Product) the value of goods and services a country produces
greenhouse gases gases such as carbon dioxide which are believed to contribute to climate change
green technology energy produced in ways that do not harm the environment, such as using wind, water or solar (Sun) power to make electricity
heritage sites somewhere – such as a building, or a forest – that has special importance, for example, because of its beauty or history
hygienic clean; promoting health
import to buy goods or services from another country
Indian National Congress the oldest Indian political party, which has formed most Indian governments since independence
inhabitants the people living in a place
invaders armies that enter another country to try to take it over
literacy the ability to read and write
livestock farm animals
middle class people who are not very rich or very poor. People who run small-and medium-sized businesses and professional people such as doctors are often said to be middle class
migration movement from one place to another
monsoon a major wind system that blows in one direction for a season, and then reverses and blows in the opposite direction. The weather varies according to where the wind is coming from – this is called a monsoon system
nepotism when those with power unfairly favour family and friends
peninsula a piece of land that juts out into the sea
population density the number of people per unit of area
sacred holy

sitar a stringed musical instrument with a long neck and rounded body

slum an overcrowded, dirty area in a town, where very poor people live

staple food the most important foods, ones that people use to make up most of their diet, such as rice

subcontinent a part of a continent that is almost separate from the rest of it

subsidise help to pay for

subsistence farming a type of farming where most of the crop is consumed by the farmer and only a little is sold for profit

sustainable capable of being maintained without using up natural resources. For example, wind is a sustainable source of energy as it will not run out

sweatshop a factory or workshop, especially in the clothing industry, where people work for very long hours for low wages and in poor conditions

tax a compulsory payment to the government, deducted from earnings, sales or property

telegraph a way of sending messages along a wire, using electrical signals

textiles (cloth) the textile industry is industry concerned with clothes, such as weaving, or making clothes

tiffin a word used in India for lunch that is brought from people's homes and delivered to their places of work. It can also mean a snack

unpaved a road that has no hard surface – just a dirt road

US Civil War a war that took place between 1861–65 between the northern and southern states of the US, mostly over the issue of slavery

vaccinating giving an injection of a weak form of a germ carrying a disease. This helps the body fight off the stronger forms of the disease

West historically describes the countries of Europle and the US

yoga exercises designed to promore physical and spiritual wellbeing

FURTHER INFORMATION

BOOKS

Journey Through: India, Anita Ganeri (Franklin Watts, 2016)

Countries in our World: India, Darryl Humble (Franklin Watts, 2013)

DK Eyewitness Travel Guide: India, various authors, (Dorling Kindersley, 2011)

WEBSITES

https://www.cia.gov/library/publications/the-world-factbook/geos/in.html
Statistics and background information about India.

http://travel.nationalgeographic.co.uk/travel/countries/india-guide/
Pictures and articles on ancient and modern India, Indian culture and travel.

http://www.actionaid.org.uk/102789/chembakolli.html
A website about life in the Indian Adivasi village of Chembakolli.

http://www.guardian.co.uk/world/india
The latest news stories from India.

INDEX